Dear Parents,

Psalty in Australia emphasizes the uniqueness of each person. Psalty the Singing Songbook's booklets search for the secret of the opal's fire and find that what makes opals valuable is the same thing that makes us valuable—God's unique plan for each of us. They learn that it's not wise to compare themselves with one another, because God made each of us different and has special plans for each of our lives.

As with all Psalty products, for this new adventure story, we've chosen struggles and concepts that affect everyone trying to live their Christian faith. We believe that if you learn these concepts as a child, they will stay with you throughout your adult years. And you will be better equipped to live a joyous life, committed to Christ.

Now snuggle close to your little one and follow Psalty; his wife, Psaltina; their booklets Rhythm, Melody, and Harmony; and their trusty dog Blooper on this eye-opening adventure in the Land Down Under.

Ernie Rettino   *Debby Kerner Rettino*

Ernie Rettino and Debby Kerner Rettino

Library of Congress Cataloging-in-Publication Data

Rettino, Ernie, 1949-
    Psalty in Australia / Ernie Rettino and Debby Kerner Rettino ; design and illustration by Dale Wehlacz.
      p.   cm.
    "Word kids!"
    Summary : Psalty and his family go to Australia to see where God's creativity worked overtime in creating an underground opal field and such animals as the kangaroo and platypus.
    ISBN 0-8499-0897-3
    [1. Australia—Fiction.   2. Christian life—Fiction.   3. Books—Fiction.]   I. Rettino, Debby Kerner, 1951-   II. Wehlacz, Dale, 1960- ill. III. Title.
PZ7.R32553Poc   1991
[E]—dc20
                                 91-497
                                   CIP
                                   AC

Printed in the United States of America

1 2 3 4 9 RRD 9 8 7 6 5 4 3 2 1

PSALTY in AUSTRALIA

Characters and Story by
Ernie Rettino and Debby Kerner Rettino

Design and Illustration by
Dale Wehlacz

WORD *kids!*

WORD PUBLISHING
Dallas·London·Vancouver·Melbourne

It was the last day of the school year . . . report-card day!

Psalty and Psaltina were planting a vegetable garden in their backyard. They were planning a surprise for their booklets. They wanted Harmony, Melody, and Rhythm to know that each booklet was very special. Blooper barked as the booklets came through the garden gate.

"Mom! Dad! Guess what?" yelled Melody. "I got straight A's on my report card." Melody waved her report card in the air as she jumped up and down.

"That's great," said Psalty.

"We're very proud of you," agreed Psaltina.

Rhythm and Harmony didn't look so happy.

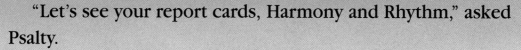

"Let's see your report cards, Harmony and Rhythm," asked Psalty.

"It's not fair!" complained Harmony. "Melody hardly even has to study and she gets straight A's. All I get are B's and C's."

"Me, Too!" agreed Rhythm. "I tried so hard to learn my multiplication tables, and I still got a D in math!"

"Settle down, everybody," soothed Psalty. "You tried your hardest, and that's all anyone expects from you. Rhythm, we'll get you some extra help with your math. And Harmony, a B is a very good grade! And if you're really trying, a C is okay, too."

"I did try hard!" Harmony insisted.

"All right, then," Psalty continued. "The Bible says in 2 Corinthians 10:12 not to compare ourselves to each other. God made each of us different. You each have special gifts and abilities. Melody is terrific at her studies. Rhythm is great at sports, and Harmony is a wonderful artist. Come on, let's not worry about report cards. Help Mom and me plant our garden."

The little booklets helped their parents dig rows for planting seeds. Blooper was also digging very hard. He was trying to find his old bones before they were covered up with string beans! Suddenly Blooper started barking very loudly.

"What is it, Blooper?" asked Psaltina.

Psalty's family gathered 'round to see. Blooper had dug up an old wooden box.

"What's in the box" asked Harmony.

Rhythm lifted the lid. "Oh! It's a small purse filled with something." Rhythm opened the purse and poured out three, milky white round stones. The stones seemed to be glowing with a colorful fire that came from within them.

"Opals!" exclaimed Psaltina. "Aren't they lovely?"

"They're beautiful!" said Melody.

"Each one of them is different," noticed Rhythm. "What makes the pretty sparkle?" he asked.

"Look!" answered Psalty. "There is a note inside the purse." The big, blue songbook pulled out the crumpled note and read:

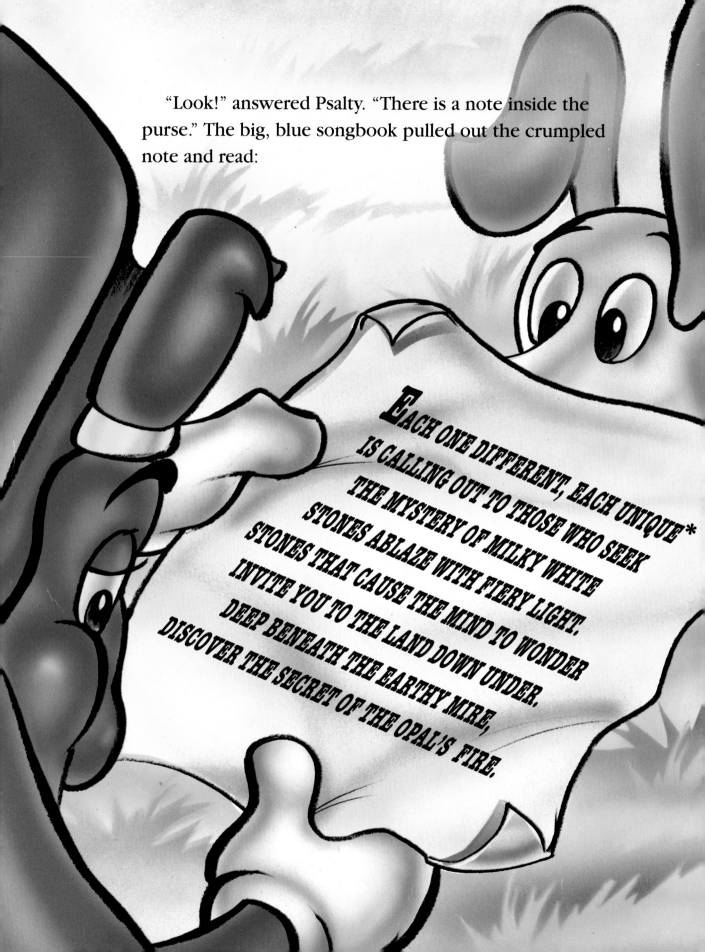

EACH ONE DIFFERENT, EACH UNIQUE*
IS CALLING OUT TO THOSE WHO SEEK
THE MYSTERY OF MILKY WHITE
STONES ABLAZE WITH FIERY LIGHT,
STONES THAT CAUSE THE MIND TO WONDER
INVITE YOU TO THE LAND DOWN UNDER.
DEEP BENEATH THE EARTHY MIRE,
DISCOVER THE SECRET OF THE OPAL'S FIRE.

"The Land Down Under? Where is that?" asked Harmony.

"The Land Down Under is Australia!" answered Melody.

"Oh, brother," said Harmony crossly, "she knows EVERYTHING."

"Booklets! Booklets!" Psalty broke in. "Beneath the earthy mire . . . that probably means underground. Somewhere underground in Australia is the SECRET OF THE OPAL'S FIRE!"

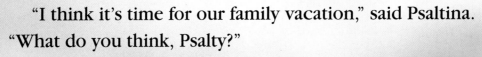

"I think it's time for our family vacation," said Psaltina.
"What do you think, Psalty?"

"I say, let's head for the Land Down Under!"

"Yippee!" they all yelled.

Psalty's family took a big jet to Darwin, Australia, the
capital of the Northern Territory.

"G'day, Mate*," said a cheerful young man when they stepped off the plane. "What brings you to the Land Down Under?"

"We're looking for the secret of the opal's fire," answered Psalty.

"The opal fields are south of here near the underground city of Coober Pedy."

"An underground city? Wow!" exclaimed Rhythm.

"Fair dinkum! . . . That's Australian for 'the real, true, and genuine thing!' My name is Outback Bob. I'm an aborigine* . . . a native Australian. Let me be your guide."

"I'm Psalty the Singing Songbook, and this is my family," said Psalty, as he shook Outback Bob's hand. "Let's get started!"

They headed off into the Australian outback* in Outback Bob's Land Rover. At first they drove through the thick, green, tropical countryside.

"I'm hungry," said Rhythm.

"Me, too!" barked Blooper.

"Let's stop and eat some tucker*. Uh . . . *tucker* is Australian for food," said Outback Bob. "I'll catch us some nice Barramundi* from that lake."

"Look at that funny little creature," Melody pointed out. "It has fur on its skin, webbed feet, and a duck bill! What is it?"

"That's a platypus*. It lays eggs like a bird, but it's a mammal*. Its babies get milk from their mother just like kittens or puppies," Outback Bob replied.

The platypus flipped its tail as it swam by.

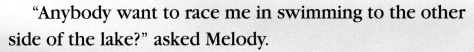

"Anybody want to race me in swimming to the other side of the lake?" asked Melody.

"Race YOU?" asked Rhythm. "Sure. Everybody knows I'm the best at sports!"

"Quit bragging, Rhythm," Harmony said. "I bet I can swim faster than you can."

"I don't know which one of you is the fastest, but keep a lookout for crocodiles," warned Outback Bob.

"Crocodiles!" exclaimed Psalty.

"Usually it's safe, but you never know. Just be careful. If you see bubbles, get out of the water fast!" said Outback Bob.

The three booklets jumped into the lake, and the race was on. Rhythm took the lead, but Harmony was gaining fast. Melody could not keep up with them. Just then, Psalty saw bubbles coming from under the water. Blooper growled. It was a crocodile headed straight for Melody!

"Melody, watch out!" yelled Psalty.

But Melody was splashing too loudly. She was trying so hard to catch up with her brother and sister that she did not hear her dad.

Psalty jumped in and swam as fast as he could to try to get to Melody in time. Psaltina prayed. Outback Bob got his rope and swung it over his head. The crocodile opened its huge jaws. Then Outback Bob lassoed the crocodile's tail. Psalty pulled Melody to safety just before the crocodile's jaws slammed shut . . . whack! That was close! Psaltina praised the Lord.

"That's enough swimming for today!" said Psalty. No one argued.

After their meal, they headed south to find the underground city.

"Look, Dad, kangaroos!" exclaimed Rhythm. "That baby kangaroo looks like he's riding in his mommy's tummy!"

Outback Bob laughed. "A baby kangaroo is called a joey. His mother carries him in a pouch. It's like a built-in baby carriage."

"If you look up in the gum trees, you might also see koalas," said Outback Bob.

"There's one!" cried Harmony. "Oh, he's so cute. He looks like a woolly little bear."

"Koalas are shy, but that one up there knows me. I call him Wally. Koalas also keep their babies in pouches," Outback Bob explained.

"God really did use His imagination when He created the animals in Australia!" said Psalty.

"Why don't I draw a picture of all of you with Wally?" Harmony said. "After all, I AM a good artist. Even Dad said so!"

"Now you're bragging, Harmony," complained Rhythm. "I want to draw a picture next. I bet I can draw as good as you."

"I can, too!" added Melody.

"Come on booklets," said Psalty. "Let's not compare ourselves to each other."

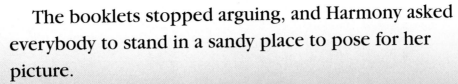

The booklets stopped arguing, and Harmony asked everybody to stand in a sandy place to pose for her picture.

"Hold still," said Harmony, as she began to draw.

"We are!" said Rhythm.

"No, you're not. You're moving," insisted Harmony.

"Oh, my!" exclaimed Psalty. "We're sinking!"

"Uh-oh," said Outback Bob. "You're stuck in quicksand!"

They were sinking deeper and deeper into the quicksand.

Outback Bob quickly tied his rope to the back of his Land Rover. Then he threw the rope to Psalty, Psaltina, Melody, Rhythm, and Blooper. They all held on while Outback Bob started up the engine and pulled them to safety.

"Praise the Lord, we're safe!" exclaimed Rhythm.

The next day, they arrived in the town of Coober Pedy. Over half the houses, stores, and even some churches were built underground! Outback Bob led them to an opal mine. They could see sparkles in the mine walls.

"A long time ago," said Outback Bob, "the sea covered this area. Sand was on the bottom of the sea. A special liquid got trapped in the sand and slowly changed into opal."

"Now we cut and polish the opals into a round shape. That way you can see the fire that glows inside them," said Outback Bob.

"So that's the secret of the opal's fire!" exclaimed Rhythm.

"God made each one of us different and special—just like the opals!" said Melody.

"It doesn't do any good to compare ourselves to each other," said Rhythm, "because we're all unique."

"That's right, Rhythm, and I like how God made me," said Harmony.

"I like how God made you, too," agreed Psalty. "And I'm glad he let me be your dad."

"Thanks, Outback Bob, for a very exciting time," said Psalty. "Now we have to go back home and see how our garden is growing."

Rhythm became suspicious. "Say, Dad, did you and Mom hide that box in our garden?" he asked.

"Yeah," said Harmony, "I bet Mom wrote the poem!"

"We'll never tell," said Psalty, as he winked at Psaltina.

GLOSSARY

Unique (yōō-nēk´) — A word used to describe something when nothing else is exactly like it.

G´day, Mate (gdā māt) — A greeting people use in Australia to tell someone hello or good day.

Fair Dinkum (fâr ding´-kəm) — An Australian term that means something is truly the real thing.

Aborigine (ab´-ə-rij´-ə-nē) — A member of the dark-skinned people who were the earliest to live in Australia.

The Outback (out´-bak´) — The country areas in Australia far away from the towns. Very few people live there.

Barramundi (bar´-ə-mun´-dē) — An air-breathing fish found in the rivers of Australia.

Platypus (plat´-i-pəs) — An animal found in Australia living near water. It has a tail like a beaver and a bill like a duck.

Mammal (mam´-əl) — An air-breathing animal with a backbone and hair. The females produce milk to feed their young.

THERE'S MORE TO COME! Follow Psalty and family's round-the-world adventures in these other great stories:

PSALTY IN THE SOVIET CIRCUS—a memorized Bible verse brings Psalty comfort when he is mistakenly thrown in jail.

PSALTY IN ALASKA—a snowy dogsled race helps Rhythm learn that we don't have to be afraid of losing if we do our best.

PSALTY IN THE SOUTH PACIFIC—being marooned on a South Seas island shows Harmony how trouble can help us grow.

PSALTY ON SAFARI—an exciting game-show win and a trip to Africa show Melody that helping with God's work can be more exciting than spending money on herself.

PSALTY IN EGYPT—a kidnapping in the shadow of the Great Pyramid ends in a lesson about the life-changing power of prayer and God's love.